KU-723-588

This Dream Book
belongs to:

For Mum and Dad,
who gave me my first box of crayons.
And for Dxo,
who kept me drawing.

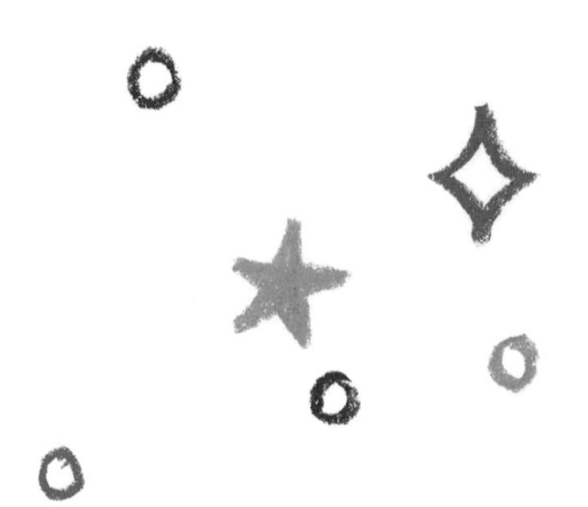

Thank you to my friends and tutors at the Cambridge School of Art, who were with me when this book was only a dream. To Lorna, Amelia and the Templar team for bringing my first book to life. To my friends and family for being on this journey with me.

A TEMPLAR BOOK

First published in the UK in 2023 by Templar Books,
an imprint of Bonnier Books UK
4th Floor, Victoria House
Bloomsbury Square, London WC1B 4DA
Owned by Bonnier Books
Sveavägen 56, Stockholm, Sweden
www.bonnierbooks.co.uk

10 9 8 7 6 5 4 3 2 1

ISBN 978-1-80078-458-1 (Hardback)
ISBN 978-1-80078-459-8 (Paperback)

The illustrations were created with wax crayons and
coloured pencils, blended with solvent, and enhanced digitally.

Edited by Amelia Warren
Designed by Chris Stanley
Production by Nick Read

Printed in China

THE
DREAM
BOOK
BIA MELO
templar
books

This is **Nina.**

She's no ordinary girl.

Most kids want to stay up past their bedtime.

But not Nina.

In fact, she **loves** going to sleep...

. . . because that's when
dreams happen!

Every night, she makes
friends with the most
extraordinary creatures.

She goes on exciting adventures
full of strange **surprises**...

. . . and is whisked away
to magical lands.
Nina **never**
wants to leave.

Yet every morning, the time comes
for her to wake up and. . .

OH NO!
The dream is **GONE!**

Nina tries her best to remember her dream. But each time, it changes bit by bit.

First it changes **shape**...

then size...

then direction...

then colour...

Until, even talking about it seems impossible.

Then poof!

She's forgotten it completely.

Don't worry, Nina. You'll have another dream tonight!
But where's my dream gone? It can't be lost. I **have** to find it!

So Nina looks here and there,
she searches **everywhere!**

Still she finds nothing.
Not even a teeny-tiny piece.

There **must** be a way
to keep my dreams!

Finally, Nina finds something that just might work. . .

...a Camera!

Tonight, she will capture her dream,

no matter what.

Fast asleep,

Nina soon finds herself

in a new adventure.

Except,

something

is wrong.

This place doesn't look so fun...

the creatures aren't so friendly...

...and it's
actually **very,**

very...

SCARY!

AHHHH!
What are you doing down there, little one? It's okay, it was only a bad dream!

Nina knows that talking about her dream is too tricky. So she has another idea instead!

Perhaps the answer has
been right there all along.
All **Nina** needs to do is capture
her dream **on paper...**

So Nina starts drawing
everything she can remember,
everything she can feel.
And it works.
At last, Nina sees her
dream in front of her.

Now every morning, as soon as Nina opens her eyes, she rushes to draw.

That way she gets to keep all her dreams – the good and the bad. And she saves them all up in a book...

a dream book,
just like this one.

TIPS FOR GROWN-UPS

How did I feel in my dream last night?

Happy | Scared | Angry | Excited | Sad

THE DREAM BOOK

Dream journalling is a great way to help children process and release emotions, understand worries, notice patterns and be creative. Journalling can also help lessen the number of bad dreams as we begin to process them in a new way.

Here are some tips to get started:

- Let them choose a new notebook to use as their 'dream book'. This can be A4 paper folded widthways and stapled, which they decorate themselves!
- Help them find a place to keep their notebook, and chosen pencil/pen, near their bed so they can reach it easily when they wake up.
- Encourage them to draw any people, animals, objects, places or colours they remember.
- Prompt them to draw a feelings chart for each dream. While dreams are a representation of emotions, it can be difficult for young children to verbalise them. Drawing a colour or emoji-like face will help with processing the dream.
- Tell them that they can talk about their dreams with you if they'd like to. They may not want to, and that's ok too.

DREAMING

Both good and bad dreams are very common for young children, especially between 3 and 5 years old.

Here are some ways to support them during this time:

- Let them know they can always call out for you or come and find you in the night.
- Explain that dreams can make you feel lots of different ways, and all of those feelings are ok.
- Remind them that dreams are not real and are just made-up pictures of things.
- Give them lots of warmth, including cuddles and reassurance, in the night and again in the morning.
- Ask the child if there is anything they need to feel safe.
- Offer them a drink of water, or to stay with them until they fall back to sleep.

BEDTIME

A child's **bedtime routine** and **bedroom environment** help to support healthy sleep.

Try these tips to create a calm, relaxing space:

- Try dimming the lights 1–2 hours before bedtime.
- Use a nightlight. If possible, use a red-toned nightlight, which helps with melatonin release for healthy sleep.
- Move around or take away certain objects in their bedroom if they are casting shadows.
- Follow a structured bedtime ritual, including: bathtime, stories and songs.
- Try a 'bad dream' spray. Use a plain water spray bottle filled with a 'potion' you can make together. This can be as simple as water and lavender oil.
- Choose a special 'sleep buddy', perhaps a cuddly toy or special charm that can be there during sleep.

Lizzie Noble is a qualified holistic sleep coach and early years educator with over 25 years' experience. More information can be found here:
www.parentingexplorers.com